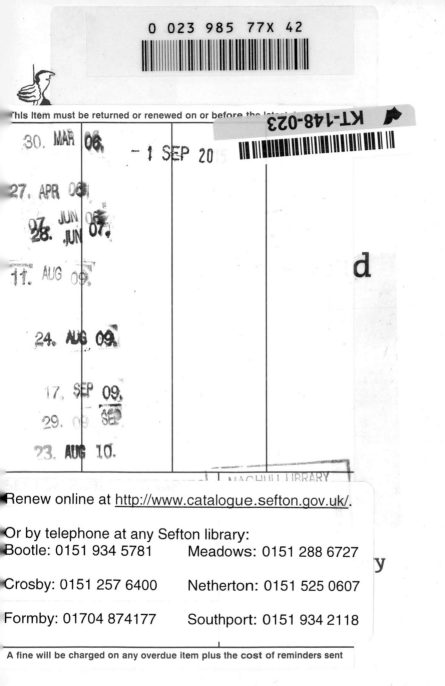

0 023 985 77X 42

KT-148-023

You do not need to read this page –
just get on with the book!

First published in 2005 in Great Britain by
Barrington Stoke Ltd, Sandeman House, Trunk's Close,
55 High Street, Edinburgh EH1 1SR
www.barringtonstoke.co.uk

This edition based on *Best in the World*, published by
Barrington Stoke in 2004

ISBN 1-842993-25-9

Printed in Great Britain by Bell & Bain Ltd

Meet The Author – Chris Powling

What is your favourite animal?
Cats. I have two at home (Jack and Max)
What is your favourite boy's name?
Jake – the name of my new grandson
What is your favourite girl's name?
Scarlett – the name of a future granddaughter (I hope!)
What is your favourite food?
Haddock and mashed potatoes
What is your favourite music?
Solo piano (all kinds ... classical to jazz)
What is your favourite hobby?
I've been a supporter of Charlton Athletic FC for over half a century

Meet The Illustrator – Martin Remphry

What is your favourite animal?
Loch Ness Monster
What is your favourite boy's name?
Edwig
What is your favourite girl's name?
Drucilla
What is your favourite food?
Curry
What is your favourite music?
Mouth organ
What is your favourite hobby?
Playing the harmonica

For Jake ...
when he's old enough

Contents

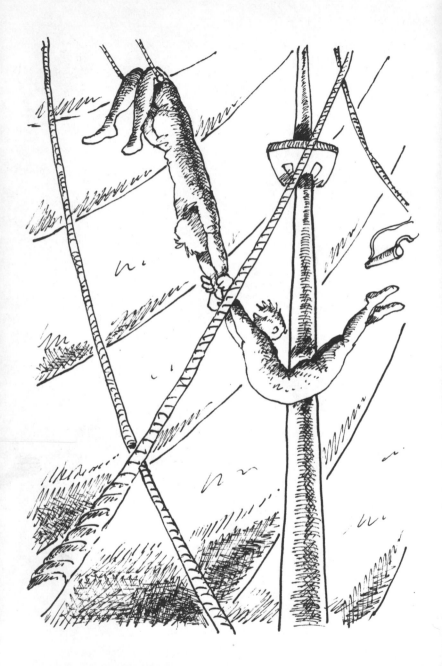

Chapter 1
Now or Never

Jeb had never been so scared.

His brother Lucas was silent as he stood on the other platform. He was swinging his trapeze towards Jeb's platform. Jeb watched it as it swung to and fro.

Down-and-up.

Down-and-up.

Down-and-up.

The gap between them looked wider than ever. So did the drop down to the circus ring. Jeb licked his lips. He must not go tense.

"Ready?" Lucas called.

"Almost ..." Jeb replied.

"Almost," hissed Lucas. "What's almost? You're ready or you're not. Which is it?"

"I'm ... I'm trying to get this right."

"Trying?"

Lucas gave a snort of disgust. "Forget trying," he told Jeb. "Just *do* it, OK?"

"Just *do* it," Jeb said softly to himself.

But he couldn't do it. Not yet. Not till his hands stopped shaking and his heart stopped thumping. He looked down at the safety net. Was it wide and strong enough? What if he missed it when he fell?

Was this how it had been for Dad?

What if I fall like Dad did?

In his dreams Jeb still saw his father's fall. Night after night, it came back to him. He watched Dad miss the safety net. Then came the crunch as he hit the ground. After that, there was silence. Dad lay broken in the circus ring. The sawdust was red with blood. At this moment in his dream, Jeb always woke up screaming.

He wanted to scream right now.

But Lucas was watching him. So was Della, their little sister. Jeb could see her peeping up at him from the back of the ring. She knew what they were doing. He couldn't back off now.

Jeb took a deep breath. "OK," he said. "It's now or never."

"Great," said Lucas. "For a moment, I thought you'd lost it. Still going for the Big One, are we?"

"The Big One," Jeb nodded.

Lucas grinned. "The Big One it is, then," he said. "After that you'll be a real flyer, Jeb. And I'll be a real catcher. Who knows, we may even get an offer from *Circusland*."

"From *Circusland*?"

"Why not? With any luck, their talent scout will come and watch us. Then they'll want our act in their show. The Big One makes you the best in the world!"

The best in the world ...

Yes, that's what the Big One made you. Everyone who's ever worked in a circus agrees about that. The Big One was what had made their father the best in the world.

Until, in the end, it killed him.

Chapter 2
The Big One

The Big One ...

That's what everyone called that great leap from trapeze to trapeze. Its other name was the Triple. You had to do three spins in mid-air at the top of the circus tent.

You had to turn head over heels backwards at terrific speed.

Three times in a row.

That's the Triple.

No wonder Jeb was scared. His timing had to be perfect when he let go of his trapeze. Any mistake and Lucas wouldn't be able to catch him. Jeb would fall like a stone into the safety net. Unless he missed it like Dad had done.

"I mustn't think like that. Just *do* it, OK?" he said to himself.

"Nice and easy," said Lucas softly.

Now they were both swinging high on their trapezes. Jeb hung the right way up – his feet pointing down to the ring. Lucas hung upside down by his knees. They needed to time it just right.

"Nice and easy ..." said Lucas.

"Just do it!" Jeb was hissing to himself.

Then he let go.

FLIP-FLIP-FLIP! went the Triple.

SMACK! went their hands as they locked together.

SWISH! went the wires of Lucas's trapeze as it carried them both to safety.

Jeb landed on Lucas's platform with a neat twist in the air. Lucas joined him a moment later. They gazed at each other. "Was that the Big One? The Triple?" Jeb asked. "Did we really do the Triple?"

"You bet we did!" grinned Lucas.

"Does that mean ..."

Lucas grinned and shook his head. "It means we're on the right track, that's all."

"But we've just done the Triple!"

"Once," said Lucas. "We've done it *once*, Jeb. Now comes the real work. We've got to practise, practise, practise till we can do it every time. After that, we can include it in our act."

"And then what?" asked Jeb.

"Then we wait for the news to get around."

"Will it get as far as *Circusland*?"

"Who knows?" Lucas winked.

"Of course it will!" someone shouted up to them.

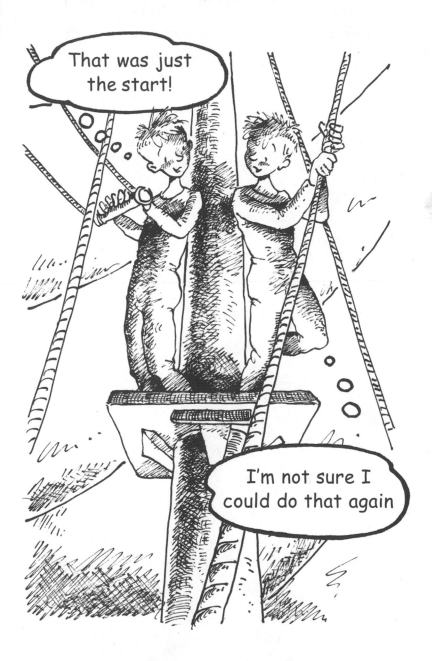

It was Della down in the circus ring. She was dressed in her clown costume for the evening show. "You're the best in the world!" she was yelling. "Do you hear that, twins? That was the most amazing trick I've ever seen! You're the best-best-best in the world!"

Chapter 3
Midnight

At last the circus was silent.

Not everywhere, of course. There were still just a few sounds. The grunts of the sleeping animals. Or the flap of the tent in the wind. And somewhere out there in the dark there was the throb-throb-throb of an electric generator. It was time to relax. Now the chatting could begin ... and the gossip.

"And what do we gossip about when we're back in our caravans?" Della grinned. "Why, it's always the same. We talk about life in the circus!"

"It's the only life we know," Mum said.

"But it's a great life, Mum!"

"So it is, Del."

Mum was brushing her red ringmaster's coat as she spoke. She did this every night before bed. The coat must be clean and smart for the next day's act. Mum kept the show together. Della knew, too, that it was Mum who'd kept the family together since Dad died.

Della bit her lip. "Er ... Mum?" she began.

"Yes, love?"

"I've been thinking about Jeb and Lucas ..."

"Go on," said Mum. "Tell me."

"They've been trying out a new trick," said Della, very fast.

"The Triple?"

"You know about it?"

"It was always going to happen one day, Del. Their dad just had to do the Triple. They're just like their dad, that pair."

"So you're not going to stop them?"

"Would you?" Mum asked.

Della thought for a moment.

She remembered how she'd felt when she was watching her brothers. The Triple had

been over in a moment. But in that moment, she'd seen the best in the world.

They were so good at it ... how could you stop them?

Mum smiled and put her arm round Della. "I have had to live with the Triple for years," she said. "You have to if you've got trapeze artists in the family."

"But isn't it risky, Mum?"

"It's the most risky trick in the circus."

"Why do people do it, then?"

"Because some people are like that. They want to test themselves. They drive fast racing cars. They climb high mountains. They rush into the sort of danger most of us would run from. The risks are part of the fun. It makes them feel more alive."

"Are Jeb and Lucas like that, Mum?"

"So are you, I expect."

"Me?"

"Don't look so amazed, Del. You've been up on the trapeze, haven't you? When you thought I wasn't looking? Trying to copy your brothers' tricks?"

"Why haven't you tried to stop me?"

"Could I have stopped you?"

"No," Della said.

"Well, there you are," said Mum. "It runs in the family. You're born to go on the trapeze. So you just have to go for it. You mustn't say no because Dad fell that time. He was unlucky, that's all. Unlucky ... and maybe a bit foolish, too."

"Foolish?"

"Dad was very tired the night he died," Mum said. "He badly needed a rest. I begged him to play safe that night and drop the Triple from his act. But he wouldn't."

"Why?"

"You see someone special had come to see him perform that evening ..."

"Who was that?"

"Someone he'd been waiting for all his life – a talent scout from *Circusland*. *Circusland* is the finest show of them all. Dad knew he was tired. But he didn't want to miss his big chance."

"But he did miss it," Della said softly.

They were both silent for a time. Mum brushed her red coat. Della sat thinking. What would Jeb and Lucas have done in Dad's place? Would they have dropped the Triple to please Mum? Or been like Dad?

What would she have done?

For once, she was glad to be away from the circus ring. The caravan felt warm and safe. She could just make out the grunts of the sleeping animals. She could hear the flap of the circus tent in the wind. And was that the swish of a trapeze?

The swish of a trapeze?

Della sat up. So that's what Jeb and Lucas were doing. Everyone else in the circus had settled down for the night. But not her brothers. Right now, in the Big Top, the twins were still working on the Triple.

Chapter 4
Last Rehearsal

Soon, everyone in the circus knew the twins were practising the Triple. "The Triple?" some of them said. "You mean the trick that killed their father?"

"That trick, yes," said one.

"But no-one does the Triple now," said another. They'll be killed as well if they're not careful."

"How can you be careful when you're spinning head over heels in mid-air?" said a third. "It's nothing to do with being careful. Jeb and Lucas have lots of talent. But their dad had too. And his talent didn't save him."

"At least he was the best in the world," they all agreed.

"For a bit, maybe. Till he did the Triple once too often. If you ask me, it's not worth the risk," said one of the clowns.

"Unless it's *Circusland* you're after," said his friend.

"Yeah ... except for that." They all nodded.

It was the dream of every circus performer to appear one day at *Circusland*, just like footballers dream of playing at Old

Trafford. *Circusland* was just as special. You had to be a top performer before their talent scout would even look at you.

Della found this hard to cope with. "It's as if the twins are doing what everyone dreams of," she told her best friend Monsieur Bonn. "Is *Circusland* so important?"

Monsieur Bonn smiled. He'd been teaching a new trick to his poodles. Now he looked up as the twins twisted and turned in the air. "Just look at them," he said. "It's beautiful, isn't it? You see skill like that and you forget how hard it all is."

"That's what Mum says," Della said, with a sigh.

Life in the circus was never easy. Some nights, the Big Top was only half full. On others, the show was held up by angry protestors. "Animal rights! Animal rights!" they yelled. Couldn't they see how well animals were treated in a circus?

There were other problems, too. Sometimes a town would ban the circus. "Who wants that kind of mess in their town?" they'd sniff. Sometimes they came to inspect the circus. Everything had to stop for this.

"Can you read, little girl?" one inspector had snapped at Della.

She didn't read much. There wasn't much time to read in the circus. But she could read. "Well, my English is better than my French," Della told the inspector, "but I do find Russian a bit hard."

That shut him up. Circus people came from all over the world.

All at once, she felt Monsieur Bonn grab her arm. "Don't look, my dear!" he hissed.

But Della had seen Jeb's mistake already. Or had Lucas got it wrong? At any rate, the twins had just crashed in mid-air. Now they were falling, falling.

Was this what had happened to Dad?

No, not quite. The brothers landed upside down in the safety net, one after the

other. They jumped up, grinning and came down into the circus ring. "See what I mean, Jeb?" said Lucas. "We needed a crash like that to get us over our fear of falling. I think we're ready now ..."

"Ready for the Triple?" asked Jeb.

"As ready as we'll ever be. We mustn't risk going stale. Let's do it for the next show."

"Tonight, you mean?" said Jeb.

"Tonight?" Della said softly.

Monsieur Bonn nodded.

He could see that the twins had made up their minds to do the Triple at the evening show. They left the tent arm in arm. They didn't even see Della, or Monsieur Bonn, or the poodles.

Chapter 5
Showtime

That afternoon it started to rain. It was still raining at teatime. By evening, it looked as if it would rain forever. "Will *anyone* come to the show tonight?" Della asked.

"Not many," said Mum. "Not in this rain."

"So the twins may not ..."

"Do the Triple? Well, it's not a good night for it, Del," Mum said. "But if Jeb and Lucas have made up their minds ..."

"They have," Della said.

Through the window she could see the lights of the Big Top. They were fuzzy through the rain. *Why not wait for a better day? Why waste the Triple on a few damp and grumpy people who were wishing they'd stayed at home?*

Lucas knew what he and Jeb had to do. "We're artists," he said to Jeb. "We do our job properly. We're paid to give our best, even if only a few people turn up."

"Do we have to do the Triple?" Jeb asked.

"That's part of doing our best, isn't it? The people who come out on a night like this deserve the Triple more than anyone! Isn't that what Dad would say?"

"Yeah, but Dad's—"

"Don't go on!" Lucas snapped.

Jeb could see that Lucas had made up his mind. And he agreed with Lucas, deep down. "OK," he said. "We'll do the Triple as planned. I only hope they see how good our act is ... the few people who bother to turn up."

He was right. Hardly anyone came to see the show that night. Only a few seats in the circus ring were full. One person had come on his own. He had some papers on his lap that he'd taken from his smart black case. He must be there because he had nothing else to do on a cold, wet evening.

Soon, even he was hooked. He was sitting on the edge of his seat.

The circus had never been more magical. It was as if they were all – the ringmaster, the clowns, the acrobats and the animals – getting ready for the Triple. You could sense it in the air. "Something special is going to happen," said a kid in the front row.

I'm scared but I can't let Lucas down

The message went from seat to seat. "Something special is going to happen!"

The twins had never felt such stress. As they came to the end of their act, they knew they had to do the Triple. There was only one way to end it now. Up on his platform, Lucas tried to think clearly. "Nice and easy ..." he told himself.

"Just do it!" Jeb gritted his teeth.

Down-and-up.

Down-and-up.

Down-and-up.

Soon, each twin was in place. Their trapezes swung closer and closer ...

At last, Jeb let go.

FLIP-FLIP-FLIP went the Big One – three fast spins in *mid-air*, at the top of the circus tent.

SMACK! Their hands met and locked together.

SWISH! went the wires of Lucas's trapeze as the brothers swung back to safety.

"Three spins?" someone yelled.

"Was that the Big One, the Triple?" gasped someone else. "Have we seen the Triple after all these years?"

It's hard for a few people to make a lot of noise – even if they have seen the best in the world. Still, they did what they could. Everyone was wildly excited. And the man

on his own jumped to his feet and cheered.
The papers on his lap spilled everywhere.

Della had never been so proud of Lucas
and Jeb. She'd never been so proud of the
circus, either.

Circusland must come and see them
now.

Chapter 6
Waiting for *Circusland*

"So, why haven't they come yet?" Della asked.

"It's only been five days," said Monsieur Bonn.

"Well that's five more Triples – six if we count the afternoon show. *Circusland* must know about it by now. Haven't they seen the reports in the newspapers? And what about all the times we've been on TV this week?"

"Wait a little longer, my dear."

Della hugged the poodles as she sat on the steps of Monsieur Bonn's caravan. "Er ... Monsieur Bonn?"

"Yes?"

"Do you think he's been here already?" Della asked.

"The talent scout?"

"He could have come any time this week," she said sadly. "Maybe they've already made up their minds that *Circusland* doesn't need the Triple."

"My dear, they can't do that."

"Why?" asked Della.

"Because *Circusland* is the best in the world. And the Triple is the best trick in the world. The two are made for each other. Lucas and Jeb have been great every single night, Della. And so have the rest of us, thanks to them!"

This was true. Somehow, the Triple had put them all in a good mood. It was as if Jeb and Lucas had made them feel special. There were more people coming to see them, too. Last night, every seat in the Big Top had been sold.

"The show ends up with the Triple!" people were saying.

"That's risky, isn't it?" said one.

"Risky? The Triple can be a *killer*," said another.

"They must have practised it for months," added a third.

"For years, more likely. You have to be very brave and time it just right. And they're only teenagers!"

"Someone told me their father ..." said one visitor.

"I heard that, too," his friend replied.

Della was scared when she heard talk like this. She'd been "warming the crowd" at the time. She had to clown up and down the gangways while the Big Top was filling up with people. The twins, and their Triple, was what everyone was talking about.

So why had no-one come from *Circusland*?

She was still sitting outside Monsieur Bonn's caravan when she saw Lucas coming towards them. He had a piece of paper in his hand. Monsieur Bonn jumped up.

Della couldn't move.

Lucas was trying to smile. His cheeks were red and his eyes were oddly bright. "It's come," he said, in a husky voice. "The letter we've all been waiting for."

"From *Circusland?*" Della asked.

"They're sending their scout to see us. He's coming to the show tonight."

"Lucas, that's great news!" said Della.

"No, it isn't," said Lucas. "It's the worst news we've ever had."

"Why do you say that?"

"Just look at me. Can't you see I'm ill? It must've been all that rain we've had. I've got a high fever. I can't breathe. My chest is on fire and my nose is streaming ..."

"You mean—"

"Della, I've got 'flu."

Chapter 7
Disaster

"Mum, stop them!" Della begged.

"I can't," said Mum. "They're just the same as their father. If they miss a chance like this they'll never forgive themselves. They'll never forgive me, either."

"But Lucas hasn't even seen a doctor!"

"A doctor would never let him perform when he's so ill, Della. And we can all see why the twins feel they can't back down ..."

"*Circusland*," Della said.

"It's the best in the world," said Mum.

"Does that make it worth the risk?" asked Della.

"What do you think?"

Della looked away. One day she might do the Triple. Anyway, she'd seen how upset everyone was when they heard that Lucas was ill. "It's only a cold," they'd said. "It won't kill him."

Well, perhaps it could.

Lucas had 'flu, remember. This is much worse than a cold.

But no-one wanted to think about that. Lucas mustn't think about it. This was the best show they'd ever done – a show fit for *Circusland*. And it was nearing the end.

Now only the Triple was left.

It was the climax of the evening. For Della and her mum, the wait was very hard. Everyone gave a sigh of relief when Lucas and Jeb began to warm-up for the Triple.

Was the warm-up taking longer this time?

Or were Jeb and Lucas dragging it out to make it all seem more exciting? Only Jeb knew that Lucas had nearly dropped him twice already. Only he could see that Lucas was hot and panting. So far they'd been lucky ... with the easy tricks.

How much longer could they put off the hardest one?

Down-and-up.

Down-and-up.

Down-and-up ...

... went Lucas's trapeze.

Yet still he went on rocking it. He seemed to be in a dream. He did not try to leave his platform.

Jeb stared at Lucas, puzzled. Lucas must know how hard it was for a flyer to keep his nerve with such a delay. Jeb was growing more and more tense. Soon he'd be unable to move. "Come on, Lucas!" he said softly.

"Come on!" shouted the crowd below.

Slowly, Lucas shook his head.

He took the safety rope. He tucked it between his ankles. He slid down to the ground. He had walked halfway across the circus ring before people understood that the show was over. There was going to be no Triple tonight.

I just can't take the risk. I might end up killing Jeb.

At first there was a stunned silence.

Then the catcalls began.

After this came wave after wave of booing.

In the end, someone threw their programme into the ring. Soon, hundreds of programmes were fluttering down like birds. The snarls and the hooting from the seats were far louder than any noise the circus animals made. In the middle of all this shouting only one person sat quite still.

It was the talent scout from *Circusland*.

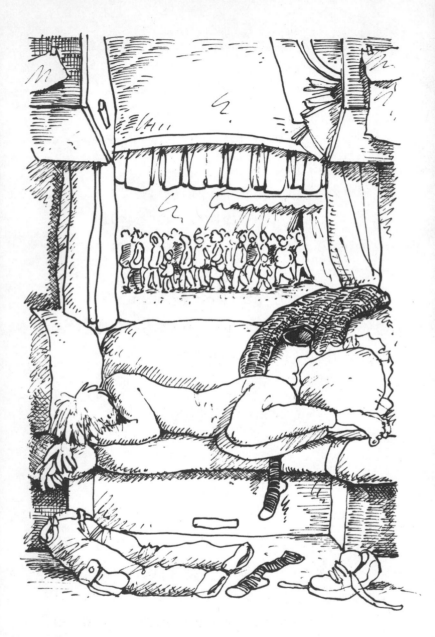

Chapter 8
Best in the World

Lucas lay slumped on a bench in his caravan. His head hurt. His chest hurt. His whole body hurt. But the hurt inside him was the worst.

Of course, no-one in the circus would blame him for what he'd done. They'd all leave him alone till he could face the world again. Even Jeb and Mum and Della would stay away for a while. "We had to get on with our jobs after the show," they'd tell him. "We couldn't come to see you. Everyone's got to clear up, after all ..."

"Not someone who's just messed up," said Lucas.

KNOCK! KNOCK!

Lucas made himself stand up. Every step he took across the caravan made his head spin. He felt sick. "Who's there?" he asked, looking out into the darkness.

"Have you a moment, young man? It won't take long. Here's my card."

"Your card?"

Lucas stared down at it. He could just about read the words in the dim light of the lamp:

```
┌─────────────────────────┐
│  ┌───────────────────┐  │
│  │                   │  │
│  │      S. Lee       │  │
│  │   Talent Scout    │  │
│  │    CIRCUSLAND     │  │
│  │                   │  │
│  └───────────────────┘  │
└─────────────────────────┘
```

"I think you've been expecting me," Mr Lee said.

Mr Lee came in. He was wearing a smart suit, and carried a trim black case, but you could see that he was used to caravans. "They tell me you're ill," he said. "Is that why you missed the Triple tonight?"

"Something like that."

"Everyone was very upset."

"Look," said Lucas sadly, "no-one was more upset than me, Mr Lee. I'm sorry if I've wasted your time."

"Who says you have? You're not the only act in the circus. Monsieur Bonn and his dogs were wonderful. So was the ringmaster – your mother, I believe. Even your little sister is great. I'm hoping all three of them will join us at *Circusland* next year."

"Really?" Lucas gasped.

"Yes, really," said Mr Lee. "But I'd still like to know more about you and your brother. It was hard to see what was going on from where I was sitting. Can you tell me what happened?"

Lucas felt ashamed. He looked away. "Everything felt wrong up there," he said. "My grip, my timing, the way I worked with Jeb. I was full of 'flu, I suppose. To begin with, I hoped that practice would get us through. Then I wasn't so sure. It seemed more and more likely that I'd drop him."

"So you dropped the Triple."

"Yes, sir."

"Quite right, too."

"Sir?"

Mr Lee bent forward a little. "Safety must always come first in a circus, Lucas," he said. "We've got plenty of problems these days without people getting hurt or even killed."

"Right ..." Lucas said.

"You shouldn't really have been out there at all tonight. You were too ill. Maybe you went ahead with the act because I was there. But you did the right thing in the end. And you were brave. It must have been hard to cancel the Triple at that late stage and in front of so many people who'd come just to see it."

"I was just so scared," said Lucas. "And it didn't help much knowing *you'd* miss our Triple as well, Mr Lee."

"But I've seen it."

"What?"

"I was here earlier this week. On a night so windy and wet that the Big Top was almost empty. You still gave your very best performance. So did everyone else in the show. I was very excited by what I saw. Did you see me? I spilt my papers everywhere."

"That was *you?*"

"It was," said the talent scout. "Tonight's visit was just to check that you and your brother have sense as well as talent. You showed me that you had."

"No kidding ..." said Lucas, in a faint voice.

"I've already spoken to Jeb and the others. They tell me they'll all be happy to join us at *Circusland* early in the New Year. Is that what you'd like, too?"

"You mean it, Mr Lee?"

"Every word, Lucas. You'll get a letter from me next week when the contracts have been drawn up. So will everyone else I've spoken to tonight. And now, you should see a doctor. That 'flu of yours needs to be attended to."

Mr Lee left soon after that. Lucas was stunned.

As he lay back on his bed, his head spun more than ever. All round him, in the dark, he could hear the circus sounds he loved so much: the grunts of the sleeping animals, the flap of the circus tent – even the throb-

throb-throb of an electric generator. Or was it just his excited heart beating?

BEST-IN-THE-WORLD

BEST-IN-THE-WORLD

BEST-IN-THE-WORLD

... it seemed to be saying.

Lucas loved that sound most of all.

Who is Barrington Stoke?

Barrington Stoke went from place to place with his lamp in his hand. Everywhere he went, he told stories to children. Some were happy, some were sad, some were funny and some were scary.

The children always wanted more. When it got dark, they had to go home to bed. They went to look for Barrington Stoke the next day, but he had gone.

The children never forgot the stories. They told them to each other and to their children and their grandchildren. You see, good stories are magic and they can live for ever.

If you loved this story, why don't you read ...

Grow Up, Dad!

by Narinder Dhami

Do you ever feel as if your dad doesn't understand you? Robbie does. His dad just doesn't know how he feels. Until one day, with a bit of magic, things change forever ...

4u2read.ok!

You can order this book directly from our website
www.barringtonstoke.co.uk

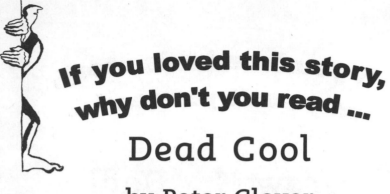

If you loved this story, why don't you read ...

Dead Cool

by Peter Clover

Do you like wacky stories? When Sammy's parents bring him home a parrot in an old, old cage, he gets more than he ever expected. Soon there are pirate ghosts all over the house, but only Sammy can see them! Can he help them to escape from their awful old captain Red Beard the Really Rotten?

4u2read.ok!

If you loved this story, why don't you read ...

Ghost for Sale

by Terry Deary

Would you like to see a ghost? Mr and Mrs Rundle buy a wardrobe with a ghost in it so that people will come to their inn, but the result is not quite what they expect.

4u2read.ok!

You can order this book directly from our website
www.barringtonstoke.co.uk

If you loved this story, why don't you read ...

Starship Rescue

by Theresa Breslin

Who can save the Outsiders from being slaves? It is up to Marc and Sasha to get a message for help to Planet Earth. But as Marc finds out, not even friends can be trusted and his task is full of danger.

4u2read.ok!

You can order this book directly from our website
www.barringtonstoke.co.uk